MARTHA'S SECRET

MARTHA'S SECRET

CAROL MOORE

SEPTEMBER 1, 2023

Copyright © 2023 Carol Moore

All rights reserved.

ISBN: -13:

Dedication

I dedicate this book to the many people who have inspired me to write this, my first novel.   I am especially indebted to my good friend Annie for buying a note pad and telling me to start writing! Also to Katee and Lyndsey who helped me to publish, and all at the Writers' Club who meet at Mulberry House, Ongar for their encouragements to get on and finish it!!

My thanks also to my husband, Ian for initial proofreading and being my listening ear.

I hope you enjoy 'Martha's Secret'.

Table of Contents

Dedication v

Chapter 1 1

Chapter 2 3

Chapter 3 6

Chapter 4 11

Chapter 5 21

Chapter 6 25

Chapter 7 28

Chapter 8 32

Chapter 9 43

Chapter 10 47

Chapter 11 54

Chapter 12 60

Chapter 13 71

Chapter 14 77

Martha's Secret

Chapter 1

The bitter wind blew through the large cracks in the parlour window, the door tap tapping. Martha sat gazing at the fire she had lit with bits of wood from a tree that had blown down.

"You can't stay here," Jonathan said, coming through the backdoor, "it's freezing outside and nearly as cold in here."

Martha knew Jonathan's wife wouldn't like her to move in with them. Jonathan was her only sibling, five years her senior. Every time he visited, the conversation was always the same, "You can't stay here, this house is falling down around us."

Their mother had died 5 years earlier. It was then that their father took to drink; he would sit in his worn chair, slouched

Martha's Secret

with his head in his hands. He hadn't been a particularly good husband, nor indeed a good father. He was unable to face the grief, over time his drinking turned to gambling. He would bring his cronies home, sitting around the dining room table. He never seemed to win and ended up by gambling all their belongings.

Hanged by the neck, life was just too much for him. They buried him in a pauper's plot.

"Go upstairs and pack, I have the pony and trap outside. I'm taking you to Ma Alice." Everyone knew her as Ma Alice, but no one was sure that was her real name.

"You're not, she's a mad witch, making potions and who knows what else in that little hut she calls home."

"Martha, she is a kind woman and I've spoken to her. Now unless you can find something better, I'm taking you there."

"No, no, I'm ok Jonathan. I'm ok."

"Well, if you won't pack, I will." At that Johnathan climbed the creaking stairs.

"No, no don't go!" It was too late; Jonathan had entered the bedroom.

"What the hell! Oh! my goodness, what…., who is this?"

Chapter 2

The stench was horrific, causing Johnathan to gag. Martha stood quietly looking at the dead man, a blanket hastily flung over him, part of his bloodied face still showing.

The room looked like a murder scene, unmade bed, blood-splattered floor and yes, the body.

"Martha, talk to me," Johnathan yelled, "What and who is this? How did he get here? What happened?"

"Johnathan, please don't yell." Martha said, by now looking quite ill. "Come downstairs please Jonathan, just leave it."

"Leave it, what do you mean leave it! There's a dead body in your bedroom and you're telling me to leave it!"

Martha went back down into the parlour, Johnathan followed still shouting, "Who? How? When? …"

Martha's Secret

Martha sat with her head in her hands, tears running down her cheeks.

"It happened the evening before father died; usual thing he and his cronies drinking and playing cards. The ship had come in from the Caribbean and half a dozen sailors arrived, most of them were drunk even before they came into the house. As usual, father was losing, but still insisted gambling everything he had, until finally he gambled me!"

I'd gone to my room; I was lying on my bed in my nightdress when suddenly the door flung open.

"You're my prize," he said. The man's face was distorted from drink.

As he approached, I shouted, "Get out of my room."

"I jumped off the bed and pushed him, it didn't take much for him to fall. I could see the blood, his eyes rolled back and I knew he was dead. I screamed so loudly that father came into my room. He swore and started calling me horrid names, by now the other men had left. I started to scream, that is until father slapped my face. I threw the blanket over the body and ran downstairs. I haven't dared to go upstairs since."

Martha's Secret

It was the following morning that Dad hung himself. When the police arrived, I prayed they wouldn't go upstairs. I told the police that Dad had lost everything he owned and he couldn't cope anymore. They left with no further questions.

"Well, that's it, you cannot stay here now. Get some things together and meet me outside in 20-minutes."

Martha, feeling sick in the stomach having seen that body again, filled a bag with her belongings and waited outside until Jonathan arrived.

"Take the pony and trap to the bottom of the lane. I'll be with you soon."

Martha did as her brother said. She watched as he carried three large cans into the house. Minutes later, Jonathan was running towards her, the house burst into flames. Johnathan took the reins and with a shout and a quick flick of the whip, they were soon far from the blazing house.

Chapter 3

Ma Alice stood waiting at the doorway of what seemed little more than a wooden shack. As Martha went into the house she was met with a welcoming fire and a large pot filled with steaming vegetables.

"Come on in lass," she said, "Sit yourself down and get this stew down you."

Johnathan thanked Ma Alice and promised to return in the morning.

The vegetable stew slipped down Martha's throat; the first real meal she had since that horrid incident in her bedroom.

"My girl you were hungry, here," as she filled the bowl up again, "there's lots more where that came from."

Martha looked at Ma Alice's face. She ain't no witch she thought, more a beautiful angel. There was only one room, a makeshift bed which was in the corner, a small wooden table with 2 wooden chairs and the armchair Martha was sitting in. In the distance you could hear bells ringing.

"There's a fire somewhere," Ma Alice said as she looked out of the door, "You can smell burning from here."

The fire swept right throughout the house. Folk was running with buckets of water; you could hear the shouting even from to Ma Alice's cottage. Martha didn't know how much Jonathan had told Alice; she didn't say anything.

"Come in deary, not helping you standing out there."

Jonathan's wife was a very hot-headed woman. She met Jonathan at the Christmas ball, run by the bank where Jonathan worked as an accountant. Rosetta was the bank manager's only daughter, so spoilt that she felt she was a cut above Jonathan's family. His mother died just a month after they married. Rosetta made it clear she wanted nothing to do with his father or his sister.

Life wasn't easy for Jonathan; his father-in-law was a hard taskmaster and insisted Jonathan worked long hours. You want to get on in this world, you need to work hard. It was made all the harder by living in the same house as Rosetta's parents. Every Sunday afternoon Jonathan would visit his sister.

Martha felt sorry for Jonathan. Rosetta was beautiful, tall and slim with natural blonde hair. Her big blue eyes and long eye lashes would flicker as she spoke. Home-life was exceedingly difficult for Johnathan. Rosetta would go riding with her friends, leaving Jonathan either at home or at work. She had her own pony and 3 cavalier spaniels who would take up much of her time. They were her children. She didn't want the inconvenience of her own children, threatening Jonathan he would need to work even more hours because they couldn't expect daddy to support them and a child.

Jonathan didn't share much about his private life with Martha but she could see he wasn't the happy-go-lucky man he used to be. As children they would spend a lot of time together, building hideaways out of anything they could find. Scrumping was another thing, hoping they wouldn't get caught while filling their pockets from next door's two large pear trees. It was one of the saddest days of Martha's life when Jonathan got married, especially after their mother had died.

Martha's Secret

"Come on Martha, come in I've made a brew. Drink it up while it's hot." Alice poured a large mug of tea for them both. Martha couldn't stop thinking of her house burning to the ground, it was the only home she had ever known. In her mind she knew she couldn't stay here with Ma Alice long term.

Looking out the door again, Martha saw the flames had died down but folk where still pouring water on the now smouldering timbers. Martha hadn't many belongings, but she had rescued the important ones, along with a few books, the tapestry she was working on, her mother's watch and a few clothes, plus her Bible.

Things where quiet at Ma Alice's. Martha helped with any chores that needed doing. It was now three days since her home was razed to the ground. A loud bang on the door startled them. It was Jonathan, looking red-faced and worried.

"Martha, get your things together."

"But Jonathan …."

"No arguing, come outside, we need to talk."

"What!" Martha looked as if she would faint.

Jonathan said, "The Police are looking for you. They found bones from that bloke and they want to question you."

Martha held onto her brother's arm. "What am I going to do, Jonathan?"

"Well, I've spoken to the captain of a ship that's leaving for Canada tonight with 150 or more folk on board, emigrating. I've got your papers; all you need to do is show them as you board the ship. Now listen, I've had to change your name your new name is Matilda Maldon.

"Who's that?" Martha yelled.

"Now listen Martha. The captain is doing me a kindness in return for…. Oh never mind, it doesn't matter. Rosetta doesn't know I have put money aside. Now you must get going, the police are searching for you and it won't be long before they visit Ma Alice's house. I don't want her getting into trouble."

Chapter 4

There was a lot of pushing and shoving as people boarded the ship, children shouted with excitement. Such was the bustle, the stewards hardly looked at Martha's paperwork as folks got on the boat, waving goodbye to their loved ones. Martha felt alone and frightened.

Johnathan had said his last goodbyes at the cottage, "I don't want anyone to recognise me or wonder why I'm seeing you off." They hugged and cried together.

"What do I do Jonathan when I get there? Where do I go?"

"You'll be told where to go when you arrive just follow the crowd. Folk will be met and taken to farms. Oh, I don't know, just follow the crowd. Now God be with you."

Martha's Secret

When Martha boarded the ship, she found a place to sit and opened the envelope Jonathan had given her. Inside was a letter and £5. She had a few coins of her own as well as a parcel from Ma Alice with a small meat and potato pie and a treacle cake.

A deafening hoot, heralded shouts of excitement as the passengers set sail on their 38-day journey. Canada had opened its borders to immigrants, inspiring thousands to look to improve their quality of life, escaping from their dismal life in England to look for opportunities in farming and mining.

Below deck, wooden beds known as berths were pushed tightly together, some stacked three high. Ventilation was poor, so folk wanted to be as close to the hatches leading to the upper decks. Martha found a single bed which pleased her. A blanket, more like sacking, was rolled up on the berth to be Martha's bed for the next 38 nights! Hygiene was poor, other than for the few who could pay for a cabin, privileged to a bowl of clean water each day. But for Martha and all the others in the lower deck, life and hygiene were an ongoing struggle.

Martha's Secret

Most folk slept in their clothes and some never changed the whole of the journey. At night, Martha would put her head under the blanket and try to sleep, made all the harder by the smell and the snoring. Martha would hold onto her Bible and pray, "Lord, please protect me." The journey was at its worst when a violent storm broke out; folk were sick and children cried with fear. Finally, shouts of delight greeted the first sight of land.

Martha had kept herself to herself, choosing not to get into conversations. After collecting their belongings everyone gathered on to the upper deck. Wrapping her stole around her shoulders, Martha, now Matilda, joined the crowd as they left the ship. They were greeted by a large poster reading, ' Welcome to Quebec, Canada'.

All around , horse-drawn carts stood waiting. The drivers shouting, "Ramsgate Mines," "Bridgewell Farm," "Cleveland Mines" …. Families rushed to get onto the carts.

"Enough!" a big man with a very loud voice shouted when each cart had filled, before telling the driver to move on.

It wasn't long before Martha realised, she was standing alone. That is until a pony and trap appeared.

"Louisa!" the man called out, "Louisa!"

Martha looked around, there was no Louisa, in fact there was no one else left!

"No Sir, I'm not Louisa, I'm Mar...... Matilda."

The gentleman stood down from the pony and trap and walked over to Matilda.

"I'm supposed to pick up Louisa."

As he came towards her Matilda realised, he was a clergyman.

"No sir I don't know a Louisa."

"Oh dear, oh dear, anyway young lady who are you waiting for?"

Tears filled Matilda's eyes, "I'm unsure sir. In fact, I have no idea where I should be going."

The man had a gentle face and a kindly soft-spoken voice.

"Well Matilda, that's what you said your name was? Didn't you?"

"Yes sir."

"Can you read? Can you write? Can you clean and cook?"

"Yes, sir," Matilda answered.

"Well you had better come with me. I'm Rev Bullingham. So, do you want to come?"

"Oh yes please," Matilda smiled for the first time in a long time.

Joseph, a handsome young, black boy jumped down and took Matilda's small trunk and taking her hand helped her on to the trap. Snow began to fall; the surrounding area began to glisten softly white.

"Wow!" Matilda thought as they drove up a long drive to a large house right next to a beautiful wooden church with a steeple and a cross on the top. This was nothing like she had seen in Liverpool. Two dogs came running up the driveway to greet them. Joseph jumped down, patted the pony then took Matilda's trunk and walked towards the house. Reverend Bullingham helped Matilda down and led her to the open door at the back of the house.

"Thank you, Joseph," Reverend said, "We shall see you at supper."

Joseph unharnessed the pony and led him to an open field next to the stables at the back of the house.

"Come in my dear, Mrs B come meet our guest. Mrs B, this is Miss Matilda. Matilda this is Mrs B my wife of many years and she still smiles," he said laughingly. Mrs B was a little lady nearly as round as she was tall, a large apron wrapped around her rotund body. Wiping her floury hands down the sides of her apron, she said, "Well, welcome my dear, but I thought your name was Louisa?"

"No my dear," Rev said, "This is Miss Matilda."

"How lovely to meet you dear. Please sit down in the parlour and I'll bring some drinks and scones."

"Please Ma'am, may I wash first? I feel so dirty after such a long journey."

"How silly of me. Yes, please do, I'll show you your room."

Matilda picked up her trunk and followed Mrs B up some steep stairs leading to a small but neat bedroom.

"This Matilda is your room and when you have freshened up come and join us for coffee and freshly baked scones."

The room consisted of a bed (covered in a colourful patchwork counterpane), a small wooden table with a jug of water, a porcelain bowl, a folded towel with a small tablet of rose smelling soap. The bleached floorboards were bare, apart from a handmade rug by the side of the bed, alongside stood a large chest of drawers with a Bible laying open on top. A small mirror hung up on the wall and a picture of Jesus surrounded by children with the verse, "Suffer the

Martha's Secret

little children to come unto me ..." hung over her bed. Matilda remembered her mother who would never hang anything over the bed, for fear it might fall and knock her out for a month!

The water was ice cold, just enough to wash her face and hands with the lovely, fragrant soap which made Mathilda feel fresh and clean once more.

Tapping on the parlour door, Mrs B said, "Come in my dear. Now sit yourself down by the fire." She gave Matilda a cup of strong black coffee along with a little dish with sugar lumps and small silver tongs.

"Help yourself, deary."

Two cups of sweet coffee and a scone, without butter but with homemade gooseberry jam, left Matilda feeling relaxed and refreshed. "I'm sorry," she said, "I've lost all track of time. What day are we in?"

"It's Thursday, 13th of May and in 2-hours it will be supper time, so go and unpack and rest awhile. You'll hear the bell when supper is ready."

""But can't I help," Matilda asked.

"Oh, tomorrow we'll have you working, now go and rest."

Supper was a large meat pie which Mrs B, wielding a large knife, cut a piece for everyone. A bowl of steaming vegetables sat on the table.

"Help yourself Mrs B," said Reverend Bullingham. He gave thanks for the food and for his dear wife for preparing it followed by a loud, "Amen" from everyone as they tucked into the scrumptious pie.

Joseph who was sitting next to Matilda poured her a glass of water, "Really nice to meet you Miss Matilda," he said, "Do you like horses?"

"Oh, yes," Matilda answered, "My brother owns a few and … Oh! it doesn't matter. Yes, I love horses."

"Then you must come and meet ours."

"Joseph loves and cares for our three ponies," Mrs B said, "He's wonderful with them. I think he loves them more than us."

Joseph gave a big smile then continued to tuck into his delicious pie.

"Would anyone like another helping?" Mrs B said.

Reverend Bullingham and Mrs B loved Joseph as their own son. God hadn't blessed them with children of their own. Joseph had been orphaned after a terrible accident on the farm where his parents worked. Tragically, they were killed along with two others when heavy timbers crushed them in a freak accident.

Joseph's parents worshipped at Reverend Bullingham's church. The Reverend took the funeral for all four – it was such a sad and solemn occasion.

Cradling Joseph in her arms, Mrs B had asked, "Is there anyone who can care for Joseph?"

"No madam," the farmer said, "I'm afraid people around here have their own families to look after."

It didn't take much persuasion for Mrs B to say they will take the child and love him as their own, and they did. Joseph always called Rev Bullingham, "Sir" and Mrs B, "Mama B."

Matilda helped wash the dishes hardly believing how blessed she felt to come to this lovely home. Joseph said goodnight, he had a room above the stables.

"You go to bed now Matilda, you'll hear the bell at 6:45, we eat breakfast at 7. You'll meet Mr Bill Stockbrook the teacher at our school which runs in the church hall. The children arrive at 8:30 a.m., you'll join him tomorrow and see how school is run."

Martha's Secret

Matilda tucked herself under the clean sheets, thanking God for caring for her.

Chapter 5

She woke with a startle as the bell rang. A quick wash and collecting her long red hair into a tight bun, she headed down to the kitchen. Everyone was sitting around the large wooden table.

"Matilda," Rev. Bullingham said, "Meet Mr Bill Stockbrook."

Mr Stockbrook stood up, "Nice to meet you miss."

Mrs B spooned out cream of wheat, a type of porridge into bowls along with mugs of black coffee. Once again Rev Bullingham stood to bless the food.

Matilda looked over at Mr Stockbrook, a man in his late twenties, tall with dark curly hair and a moustache. She also noticed he only had one arm, trying hard not to stare, she wondered how he had lost it. Mr Stockbrook had grown up on his parents' farm. There wasn't much he didn't know about farming; from a young child he would get up early and help milk the cows. They also grew wheat on the large farm inherited from his grandparents. Mr Stockbrook loved farming but also loved studying English and mathematics. A local teacher, Mr Thomas Coleman would visit twice a week to teach young Bill.

He learnt to play the violin and would often play to entertain the farm labourers at the end of Harvest. He'd known Mary Blair since they were children, a second cousin of Bill's mother who owned the neighbouring farm, they had 5 daughters, Mary being the eldest.

On Sunday after Chapel, that's when Bill and Mary would walk together by the lake. They would often sit under the maple tree where Bill would read poetry to Mary. It was no surprise when the two got married. And what a wonderful wedding! Bill played the fiddle while folk sang and danced. Mary moved house into Bill's family farm; everyone said they were the loveliest couple.

The church was full and not a dry eye among the many mourners. Tragically their baby was born dead, the boy looked perfect . The doctor said he couldn't do anything for

Mary, she had lost so much blood. Bill sat holding her cold hand and watched the life disappear from her beautiful body.

There were no charges brought the day Bill fell through the baker's shop window.

"His punishment was enough," Mrs Emma Bradwell said, "He's lost his wife and baby and now his arm as well. If he pays for the repairs to the window, we'll say no more."

"Drink's the Devil's poison," Bill's mother said as she nursed him, "It never solves anything."

Bill tried to close his ears to his mother going on about the evil drink. With the grief for his wife and baby along the loss of his left arm, Bill Stockbrook fell into a deep depression wondering what he would do with his life. He couldn't help on the farm anymore and dreaded the thought of just sitting in the parlour hearing his mother droning on. He began to think the only way was to end his life.

Bill couldn't remember how he ended up knocking at the Reverend Bullingham door. They sat drinking coffee and talking for what seemed hours. "Well young man, what do

Martha's Secret

you think? I've longed for a school for the underprivileged children for years. Will you take the work on? Will you teach these farm workers' children.

Chapter 6

Joseph was still ringing the bell as the 22 children filed into class; their ages ranged from 4 to 12 years old.

"Good morning, children," welcomed Rev. Bullingham, "We have a new teacher to help Mr Stockbrook, this is Miss Matilda."

Matilda loved working with the children, teaching the young ones on one side of the classroom while Mr Stockbrook taught the other older ones on the other. It had been nearly three months since Matilda had arrived at Reverend Bullingham's rectory; how blessed she felt. When she had time, Matilda would see Joseph; she grew to love him as a brother.

Matilda wrote to Jonathan and Ma Alice knowing it could take anything up to 8 weeks before the letter would arrive.

How she longed to hear from her brother; she missed him but knew deep down she might never see him again.

The police had stopped the investigation, thinking that even she may have died in the fire. Jonathan would occasionally visit Ma Alice. Martha was never mentioned and Ma Alice, being a wise woman, knew it was none of her business but in her heart she missed Martha and often wondered what she was doing. Ma Alice and Jonathan were thrilled when the post eventually arrived, a letter for each of them.

"Dearest brother, I am well and blessed. I'm living with Rev. Bullingham and his dear wife, they are so kind to me and I feel part of their family. I'm helping Mr Bill Stockbrook at the school in the church. I so enjoy teaching the little ones to read and write. It gets cold at night; we have snow here but I have a cosy warm bed and Mrs B. ensures we have lots of hot drinks. I do miss you and pray for you every night. Please write and tell me how you are. Now dearest brother, sending you my deepest love, Martha."

Martha's Secret

"Dear Ma Alice, I'm happy and living in a lovely home with the Reverend Bullingham and his dear wife. I know you would love her. I will always thank God for the way you cared for me when life was difficult. I do hope you are keeping well, if you can write to me I'd love to hear from you. I think and pray for you often, please pray for me too. Regards Martha."

Chapter 7

Mr Stockbrook closed the classroom door, "See you in the morning miss Matilda."

He wrapped his coat and scarf around him and walked back to the farm. It was about half an hour's walk away; he enjoyed the walk after being in the cramped classroom all day.

Matilda watched as he walked down the lane. How she loved working with him in the school. In fact, she loved just being with him, sometimes after school they would walk to the park together, talking about the children and the schoolwork, sometimes when he smiled her tummy would turn over; a strange feeling she thought. She knew she was beginning to have feelings for him, feelings she didn't really understand. She missed him terribly at the weekend, although Mr Stockbrook did come to Chapel where he would sit with his parents while she sat at the front alongside Joseph.

Matilda turned to go back to the house, she saw a young woman speaking to the Reverend . She capped her ear as she listened to their conversation.

"I'm sorry I didn't arrive on the boat three months ago. I went down with a fever but I'm fine now. I did write but I expect it hasn't arrived yet."

"Louisa, now this is a surprise but do come in," Reverend Bullingham said. Matilda stood shaking, feeling her entire world had just fallen apart. It can't be, but yes it was Louisa Springfield, Constable Springfield's daughter from the village Martha lived in . Matilda felt sick; she ran up the back stairs to her room with tears rolling down her face. Matilda packed her small trunk and wrote a short note,

'My dearest Reverend and Mrs B, I must leave immediately, I need to get to a town far from here to see an old aunt who is dying. Please forgive me for not coming in to see you first but I noticed you have a visitor and I must rush to get to the Coach House. Thank you and

know I will always be grateful for all you have done for me. Regards, Matilda.'

How she hated telling lies, her mother always said lying was a wicked thing. Matilda ran to the stables.

"Joseph, Joseph, where are you?"

Joseph came running, "What's up miss Matilda? Why have you got your trunk?"

"Please don't ask questions Joseph. I just need you take me to the Coach House. But…. but Joseph, please do not ask, just give this note to the Reverend."

It only took 20 minutes to arrive at the Coach House; people mingling around, coachmen drinking beer, leaning on the wall of the Coach House. Joseph helped Matilda down, his face confused but he didn't ask questions.

"Bless you dear Joseph. Don't forget to give the note to Rev and Mrs B."

Matilda turned her face away so Joseph wouldn't see the tears beginning to run down her cheeks. Once again, Matilda felt alone and afraid.

"Need help miss?" one of the coachmen asked, being aware Matilda looked lost.

"Where are you going, please?" she asked.

"St Johns."

That meant nothing to Matilda, but she replied, "And how long will that take?"

"Four hours, I don't rush my horses."

"No, that's fine thank you. "Have you room for me to travel?"

"Yep! leaving in 15 minutes."

The man took Matilda's trunk and put it on roof of the carriage. Taking out her purse and paying what the man asked, Matilda stepped inside the carriage. After a while, two elderly ladies and a rather large man joined them.

The driver and a young boy climbed up, took the reins shouting, "Get up now!"

The journey had begun.

Chapter 8

"What do you mean she said nothing," Mrs B said, reading the note Joseph handed her. "Did she say where she was going? and who is this aunt, she never mentioned before. You should have called us, Joseph."

"Ok dearest," Rev Bullingham said, "It's not Joseph's fault. I'll take the pony and trap into town and see if she is still there."

No one wanted to eat much at supper, other than Louisa who tucked into a bowl of steaming stew. Louisa was shown to a room right next to the one Matilda had and just as clean and welcoming, but Mrs B didn't have the joy she had when showing Matilda to her room. Lousia unpacked and lay on the bed. The long journey on the boat had taken its toll on her, her head was spinning. Perhaps she had eaten too much, that delicious stew was now gurgling in her tummy. Without even undressing, she pulled the knitted blanket over her head and fell into a deep sleep.

The journey was slow, the snow was falling more heavily now. The two women never stopped chatting while the portly man slept, snoring throughout. Matilda kept dabbing her eyes to prevent the tears falling down her cheeks.

"Oh Lord, of all the people to arrive at the house, why her? why Louisa?"

In the three months Matilda had spent with Rev and Mrs B Matilda she had almost forgotten the horror of what had happened that dreadful night in her bedroom. As the coach came to its destination, fear came over Matilda like never before. Taking hold of her trunk, she followed her fellow travellers into the inn. Matida paid the innkeeper and was shown to a shabby and not particularly clean room. Pulling the covers down, she shuddered as she saw bed bugs scuttling away as she shook the sheets. Exhausted by the day's events, Matilda pulled a torn blanket around her praying the bugs wouldn't bite her in the night.

Lousia was startled by the bell, and rushed to join Rev, Mrs B, Joseph and Mr Bill Stockbrook for breakfast. Bill Stockbrook couldn't believe his ears when the Rev told him Matilda had left. He quickly turned his face away, with a sinking feeling in his heart.

"Pull yourself together," he said to himself.

"Good morning, Miss Louisa. I hope you enjoy your stay at the school. The children will be arriving in 15 minutes, so shall we prepare for them to arrive?"

The children kept asking questions of Mr Stockbrook, "Where is Miss Matilda, sir? Oh, we will miss her. Is she coming back?"

"Be still children, the Rev is coming to pray with us."

"Good morning children, before we thank our Lord for a new day, I want you all to meet your new teacher, Miss Lousia. I'm sure you'll make her feel welcome."

"But I only want Miss Matilda," one small boy cried.

"Dear Lord, thank you for a new day. Please help miss Louisa as she settles into our school," and with a choke in his voice continued. "Please keep Miss Matilda safe and well. Amen."

Matilda walked out of the inn, the town was buzzing people pushing carts carrying all kinds of vegetable and fruit going to the open market. Matilda had no idea where she would go but knew she would have to look for work. She had managed to save some of her wages plus most of the money her brother had given her, but Matilda knew her savings would soon dwindle. She left her trunk at the inn and told the innkeeper she would return later.

"That's fine," he said, "But I take no responsibility for it. If it goes, it goes."

Matilda walked through the open market, buying herself a loaf of bread. It smelled good and was still warm. Walking out of the market into open fields, Matilda sat down and broke pieces of the warm bread, realising just how hungry she was. The taste was wonderful, but nothing like sitting at the breakfast table with Mrs B, the Reverend and dear Joseph, oh! and Mr Bill Stockbrook.

After tucking into nearly half of the loaf, Matilda started walking back towards the market. It was then she noticed a group of children running across the field, all neatly dressed and carrying what looked like books tied with string.

"Good morning children." Matilda was able to catch them up. "Where are you all going?"

The biggest girl, probably 10 years or so, stopped and answered, "School, Miss."

"And where is your school?"

A young girl pointing, said "Over there, Miss."

"May I walk with you?" Matilda asked, "I would like to speak to one of your teachers."

"We haven't done anything wrong," one child yelled.

"Oh no, I just want to speak to teacher. You haven't done anything wrong." Matilda smiled at the frightened looking child.

The school was across the field, there were six small huts, freshly painted bright green.

"There miss, this is our school."

The children ran on as the bell was being rung by an older child. "Come on you lot, get to your classes," he yelled.

Matilda walked up to one of the huts where a smartly dressed, middle aged teacher came out who looked Matilda up and down; Matilda realised how unkempt she looked.

Martha's Secret

"Can I help you?"

Matilda approached the smartly dressed teacher, "Oh, why have I come here? Why didn't I do my hair and put a different dress on?" These thoughts ran through Mathilda's mind as the teacher stood staring at her.

"Well, have you any qualifications? Have you ever taught before?

"Yes, ma'am," Matilda now shaking, replied, "I taught at Rev Bullingham's school for nearly four months."

"And have you references or papers to prove you are a teacher?"

"No, I'm afraid not, I had to leave in a hurry, an aunt of mine became extremely ill. I didn't have time to ask for references, but I enjoyed teaching and the children seemed to like me."

The teacher smiled politely, "I'm sorry my dear, we are renowned for good teaching here and sadly you have nothing to show me you have taught." Looking straight at Matilda, "We also have a high standard of dress code."

"Oh, please if you could just give me a chance. I'm sure I can show you I am a good teacher."

Turning to go into her classroom, the teacher replied, "We don't need any more teachers, I wish you good day." She closed the door behind her, leaving Matilda standing wondering whatever she would do.

"What do you mean, it's not here?"

"I told you; you could leave your trunk but I couldn't guarantee it would still be here."

Matilda looked around at the folk sitting drinking at the large wooden tables, "Has anyone seen my trunk please?"

It was noisy, people laughing and shouting, it seemed no one heard Matilda's distressed cry.

"Come and sit here," one man said, full of beer. He could hardly stand but he was still able to slap Matilda on her backside.

"How dare you," she cried, which only caused more laughter.

Matilda made her way back to the market in the hope of finding something to eat. The stall holders were clearing away, some had even gone. Unable to hold back the tears Matilda leaned against a wall the tears streaming down her face.

"Hey child, what's up? What's making you so sad?" It was the lady who sold Matilda the bread earlier in the day.

Sobbing she cried, "Someone has stolen all my belongings. I don't know where to go or what to do."

"You're English, ain't you?"

"Yes ma'am, I came over more than four months ago. I was working as a teacher, but I had to leave."

"Had to leave, what did you do?"

"Oh, nothing like that, in fact they were wonderful to me."

"Well, can't you go back?" Still sobbing, Matilda didn't answer, thinking only if she could go back.

"Well, dry your tears, Jack will be here soon with the cart, most of the folk here work in the fields. It's harvest time and they are always looking for workers and you'll find many are from England too."

"Have you any bread left?" Matilda asked, "I can pay, I have my purse with me, thankfully I never put that in the trunk."

"No love, all sold first thing this morning. Come along I'll introduce you to Rosie, she works at the farm."

"Mary Ann!" the women shouted to a woman packing second hand clothes away, "Young women, What's your name, love?"

"Matilda," she replied.

"Matilda has had all her belongings stolen." Mary Ann sorted out two dresses.

"Here dearie, these should fit you." One was a drab grey dress that Ma Alice would have worn and the other a pretty green dress with a frill around the neck.

"I'll pay," Matilda said.

"Don't worry dear, they were old James' Gran's. She died few weeks back, you have them."

Rosie shouted. "You joining us dearie? If so, jump in the cart."

It was a large cart drawn by a poor looking thin horse. About 8 folks got in the cart, and with a loud shout, 'gee up!' the cart was on the move, along unmade roads, to the farm. Matilda watched the man unharness the horse and lead him to the open field. She looked at the poor animal and thought of Joseph and how he cared for his ponies.

Matilda followed everyone into a large barn, a big makeshift table with bales of hay to sit on.

"Sit yourself down Matilda, I'll tell Jack you're here."

"Is he the owner?" Matilda asked.

"Oh no, no, jack is the foreman. He's tough but fair."

"Sorry," Matilda said, "But I don't know your name."

"Rosie, but that's not my real name, everyone calls me Rosie due to my red cheeks," she said laughing.

"So, you want a job" Jack said, standing head and shoulders over Matilda, "Well, we are always looking for folk willing to work hard at harvest."

"I'll work hard, sir," Matilda said.

"Ha, ha no one calls me sir," Jack said, "but I want to tell you what most call me. Aye Rosie."

Rosie laughingly said, "Take no notice dearie. Ok sit yourself down and help yourself to some grub."

Matilda took a tin plate and some bread and a slice of very fatty meat, she had no idea what meat it was and chose not to ask, along with a tin mug filled with lukewarm tea. It all went down well as she was so hungry. The barn was filled with laughter and shouting, everyone talking over one another, but Matilda sat quietly just wondering whatever was going to happen to her. She felt grateful she had food and work, yet sad that she wasn't staying with Reverend and Mrs B. Oh, how she missed them.

Chapter 9

Reverend Bullingham walked through the back door where Mrs B was busy baking a cake for Joseph.

"I have walked everywhere but no one has seen Matilda. I'll go again tomorrow and then we will have to accept she has left us. I just cannot understand it, it's just not like her to walk out and who is this aunt? She has never mentioned her to us before."

Louisa had just arrived, back from school.

"Is that Matilda you're talking about," in quiet a cruel tone. "That's all I ever hear at school from the children. 'When is miss Matilda coming back. and Mr Stockbrook hasn't smiled since I arrived.'"

"Now don't talk like that Louisa," Mrs B said, "She was, or I should say is, a sweet loveable young lady and we are all concerned for her whereabouts."

"Well, it's not making things easy for me Mrs B, and to be honest this isn't the kind of work I thought it would be."

Reverend Bullingham looked up from his book which he sat reading while drinking his cup of coffee, "Are you unhappy here Louisa?"

"Not really," Louisa answered, "but there is no one my age to talk to and the only outing I have is when Joseph takes me into town."

A tear ran down Louisa's cheek.

"I wish I'd never come here," she cried, "My parents felt it would help me to get over things by coming to Canada."

"Get over what things dear?" Mrs B asked, coming alongside Louisa and placing an arm around her shoulder. Louisa put her head in her hands.

"I loved him, really loved him but they sent me away to my mother's spinster cousin. I didn't really have a fever; I had a baby. I never saw her, they came along and took her, the nuns that is. 'It's for the best' they said, 'she will be loved and cared for as their own'. I don't know where they took her and when I came home my father told me he had written to you in response to your advertisement and the rest is history. I know it's not your fault but well, I feel alone."

"Oh your poor dear child," Mrs B hugged her all the more. "Only if miss Matilda had stayed, I'm sure you two would have got along so well."

"To be honest, Mrs B and Reverend. Alfred wanted to marry me. I received a letter from him before I left."

Louisa took a well-read letter from her slip, "You can read it," she said, giving it to Reverend Bullingham.

'My love they are trying to tear us apart but my heart longs for you. I haven't a fortune or prospects, only a heart full of love for you. I will wait as long as it takes for you to return to England. We could get wed next year when we are both of age. We can travel to Wales, start afresh, there is always work on the sheep farms. I'll wait for you my love, your Alfred'.

Reverend Bullingham and Mrs B sat silently looking at Louisa as tears flowed down her cheeks.

"It's now five months since I left England and Alfred; I can never find happiness without him."

"You must do whatever you think is right," Mrs B eventually said, "If you wrote to Alfred now, he would get it by Christmas."

"I've been deceitful to you both; I have already written to him, two months ago, but I haven't heard back yet."

Louisa was sobbing uncontrollably, Mrs B was holding Louisa close to her bosom, her pinny now wet with tears.

Reverend Bullingham did what he always did in times of upset; he knelt placing his hand on Louisa head and prayed that the good Lord would comfort and help her.

Chapter 10

Work was hard on the farm. A whole month had passed, Matilda's mind often drifted back to thinking about the Reverend and the school. How she missed them all. Everyone was friendly at the farm, especially Rosie but it was no answer to the pain she still carried.

Christmas decorations were being put up in the school; the children were so excited as Reverend Bullingham dressed as Santa Claus coming into the classrooms with a gift for each child. Folk in the church had been very generous and made something for each of them. There where knitted gloves, wooden spinning tops, skipping ropes and Mrs B had made each child a cookie iced with their name on.

Martha's Secret

It was less than a week since Louisa spoke to the Reverend and Mrs B when she walked into the parlour with a big smile on her face, almost stretching from ear to ear.

"I've heard from Alfred; our letters must have crossed. He wants me to go back and travel with him to Wales. Oh, please read it Reverend."

'My mother's brother Thomas has moved to Wales; he says the farmer will take me on too. There's also work in the big house, so we could be together. I'll keep waiting at the harbour until you return. I long for that day. Your beloved, Alfred.'

Reverend Bullingham took Louisa to the dock and booked a trip on the next ship going back to England.

"That's five days' time," the man said, "$25 dollars second Class or $50 if you want a single cabin."

"I've saved all my money," Louisa said, "I have got almost $35."

"Ok $35, but you'll have to share a cabin."

On 20th December 1901, Louisa boarded the ship for Liverpool. The night before, Mrs B had baked a large apple turnover, wrapped it in brown paper and gave it to Louisa for the journey.

"We wish you every blessing," Reverend said, "Joseph will take you to the dock."

When Joseph returned, the Reverend told him he wanted him to go to the coach house and travel to St. Johns.

"There's a parcel I need picking up and I'd like it before Christmas morning."

Joseph never questioned or argued. He brought the pony and trap around and waited for the Reverend to step up and take the reins. Rev dropped Joseph in town to catch the next coach to St John's. The passengers didn't speak for much of the journey but together they sang Christmas carols, laughing at their out-of-tune voices. Joseph however, slept for most of the journey.

St. Johns was bustling with people, Joseph walked straight to the cathedral, which was standing majestically in the middle of the town. As he walked in, he was greeted by the Right Reverend Toby. Toby in name and tubby in statue, fully robed unlike Reverend Bullingham who only robed for funerals and weddings.

"You must be Joseph," he said, "I received a letter for Stergan."

Joseph had never heard anyone even Mrs B call the Reverend by his Christian name.

"Must have been a long journey for you, Joseph."

Joseph hoped he may have been offered some refreshments, but instead he was just handed the parcel tied with a piece of string.

"I'm sure you want to get the next coach back, so I'll bid you good day and a blessed Christmas to you."

Joseph was pleased he bought his purse with a little money, at least he could go to the inn and get a drink and something to eat. He walked back to the coach house.

"What time will you be leaving?" he asked the coach driver.

"Blimey mate, you've only just arrived! Won't be till 4 o'clock, You've got over two hours yet."

The hot soup satisfied Joseph's hunger but it was nothing in comparison to Mrs B soup, nevertheless it was hot and a thick slice of bread.

"Lovely bread," Joseph said to the lady serving him.

"Yes, bought it fresh this morning from the market; make lovely bread they do."

Martha's Secret

Matilda arrived early that morning at the market, she helped set up the stall with freshly picked turnips, carrots and a few parsnips. Mary Ann had her usual stall cluttered with second-hand clothes. The bakery always sold out quickly, folk loved the freshly baked bread. One stall had Christmas decorations and sweets wrapped in pretty paper bags, homemade fudge and coconut ice, slabs of treacle toffee and much more. Matilda bought herself a stick of nut brittle, sucking it throughout the morning, even as she served her regular customers.

"Time to pack up," Rosie shouted across the stalls, "haven't got anything left here, how about you Matilda?"

"Just a few turnips."

"Drop erm on the floor Tilly, some poor sod will pick them up."

Rosie was the only one who called Matilda, Tilly. Matilda thought it quiet endearing. She liked Rosie as she always looked out for her and made sure Matilda had all she needed.

The cart had arrived, Jack shouted, "Come on ladies, let's get going it's been a long day."

Joseph left the inn; he still had an hour before his journey home. He walked slowly towards the open market and watched folk dismantling their stalls. Only Mary Ann was still serving, women and children rummaging through clothes, hoping to find something to fit.

"Come on you lot," she shouted, "I've a home to go to."

Joseph looked on smiling to himself as he saw a large lady holding up a dress two sizes too small. It was then his eyes caught site of the cart. Could it be? It was! Joseph ran as fast as his legs could take him but the cart was far away.

"Matilda, Matilda."

Matilda looked around and saw Joseph in the distance. She quickly hid her face; pain struck her heart.

"Oh Joseph," she sobbed, "How I miss you."

"Hey girl" Rosie said, "Why the tears?"

Rosie knew when not to push for answers.

Joseph ran back to the market where only Mary Ann was there, bundling the unsold clothes into a sack.

"Sorry love, I'm done for the day."

"No I don't want to buy anything; I'm just wondering if you knew where the people on the cart are going?"

"Oh, Rayburns Farm. Why? Are you looking for work?"

"No I'm looking for a friend, Matilda. Do you know her?"

Mary Ann gave Joseph a strange look.

"No dearie," pushing him aside, "Now excuse me I need to pack up or I'll never get home."

Chapter 11

Jack walked to the barn. "Matilda, get yourself cleaned up and put this apron on they need help in the kitchen at the big house."

And it was a big house; the owner lived there with his only son.

"It's only until the Christmas celebrations are over. You work with cook, just do as she tells you and you'll be fine."

Matilda walked into the kitchen. She had never seen anything like it in her life! A great big range, pans of every shape and size hanging from some wooden contraption from the ceiling and a big pine table where cook was rolling pastry. Cook barely looked up as Matilda walked through the door.

"The washing up needs doing, it's in the scullery next door."

Two big butler sinks filled with pots and pans and lots of crockery. Matilda sorted everything out, filled one sink with hot water from an urn.

"Matilda!" cook called out, "take this tray to Mr Albert."

A tray with a pot of tea, milk and sugar and a plate with two freshly baked current buns. Matilda knocked on the big wooden door, putting the tray down on a large highly polished sideboard with freshly cut flowers in a beautiful cut-glass vase.

"Come in!" Matilda, having put the tray down, went to leave.

"Pour it girl."

Mr Albert was a tall handsome man, probably in his early 40s, he seemed very unkempt; egg from breakfast down his shirt, the smell of whisky was overpowering as he came close to her. As Matilda poured the tea he came behind her, cupping Mathilda's breasts in both hands.

Matilda shouted, "What do you think you're doing?"

Feeling his breath on her neck she flew round spilling the boiling tea over his bare arm.

Martha's Secret

"You stupid girl" he shouted, slapping her face hard making Matilda scream. She pushed him away as cook came running in.

"Get her out!" Albert shouted, "Get her out!"

Matilda ran back to the barn still screaming, her left eye nearly closed from the blow. "Not again, Lord not again!"

Joseph arrived back with the books; it was late but Rev Bullingham had waited up for him.

"Oh, dear Joseph, if I'd known the time of the coach I would have met you."

"It's ok sir, but I must speak with you."

"Oh Joseph, it's late, speak in the morning."

"Please sir, listen to me; I've seen Matilda."

Reverend Bullingham quickly turned, staring at Joseph, "You saw Matilda? Where?"

Joseph explained how he saw Matilda on a cart leaving the marketplace and was told it was going to a farm.

"Oh sir, I tried so hard to call her. I asked if anyone knew her. I did get the name of the farm - Rayburn Farm."

Reverend Bullingham thanked Joseph, "Get yourself to bed now and we will talk in the morning."

Matilda put her few belongings in a sack.

"Wait" Rosie said, "What's going on?" Looking at Matilda's swollen eye, "Has that swine started his tricks again?"

"I'm leaving," Matilda said, "He's thrown me out."

"Not this time of night, you're not. Now get to bed"

"No, I'm going."

"Please Tilly, wait till morning. Jack will run you into town. Where will you go?"

Matilda didn't answer because she had no idea where or what she would do.

She didn't sleep much that night. Rosie poured her a cup of tea and told her Jack was waiting in the cart.

"Will you go back to that Reverend bloke you spoke about?"

"I'm not sure, but don t worry about me Rosie, you have been a real friend to me."

"Oh, shut up" Rosie said with a tear rolling down her cheek, "Now you take care of yourself."

Martha's Secret

Matilda climbed onto the cart.

"Come up front with me, Matilda," Jack said.

Matilda's eye was blackened and the finger marks still evident on her cheek.

"I know what I'd like to do to that son of a ….."

"Please don't," Matilda said.

Jack released the reins and the horse was off down the lane. Jack didn't say another word.

"Tomorrow is Christmas Eve," Rev said at breakfast, "I have visits and need to prepare for the service tomorrow and Christmas day. We will have to wait until next week before we can try to find Matilda."

Mrs B sat at the table her head in her hands.

"Whatever is that girl doing working on a farm? Do you think she is in some sort of trouble?"

"There, there," Rev said, "We will try to find her. Now where's our breakfast?"

"Sir," Joseph exclaimed, "Today is the last day the coach goes to St Johns. Please let me go. If I am quick, I can get the early coach."

Martha's Secret

Jack stopped at the market. A few stalls were setting up but Matilda didn't look up. She didn't want to see anyone she knew, knowing Mary Ann would start asking questions. Jack put an envelope into Mathilda's hand.

"This is what's owed you, sorry it's not more."

"Thank you for everything Jack, everyone has been so kind to me."

Jack helped her down and without a word he got back up and with a little tug of the reigns set back to the farm.

Mrs B was serving breakfast when they heard a knock on the door.

"Good morning!" Bill Stockbrook stood by the doorway, "I've some papers I want to pick up, I won't disturb you."

"No, do come in," Reverend said, "Join us for breakfast. Joseph has some news about Matilda."

"I'll come with you Joseph," Bill said when he heard Joseph was travelling to St Johns.

"I would like to help to find Matilda. Seems things aren't as they should be - working on a farm ..... Well, we'll need to get a move on and pray there will be room on the coach."

Chapter 12

"You're lucky, two spaces left, but it will cost you and extra 'cos it's Christmas!"

Joseph and Bill got into the carriage.

"Any idea what time you'll return?" the Rev asked, "Oh not late tonight, about 8.30 or so."

"That's grand," Reverend said, "I'll be here to meet you with our pony and trap. God speed and I'll be praying you will find out what's happened to Matilda."

"What now, Lord!" Matilda said aloud, "What now?"

The streets were starting to get busy; the wind was bitterly cold on Mathilda's still sore face. As she walked by the cathedral, she noticed two ladies going through the door.

Martha's Secret

"Excuse me," Matilda said, running towards them, "Please may I come in?"

The two ladies looked at one another.

"We're only here to clean dear, but I'm sure if you want to come to pray Reverend Toby wouldn't mind."

Pray, Matilda thought. She sat down on one of the pews her head in her hands.

"Ok God, what am I to do?"

She wasn't sure how long she had been sitting there when Rev Toby came and placed his hand on her shoulder.

"Are you alright" he asked gently, it made Matilda jump, she hadn't heard him come over to her.

"Oh, oh yes, thank you I'm Ok......"

Looking at the swollen black eye, Rev Toby asked, "Are you in trouble?" Seeing the sack which held all her belongings.

"Are you running away?"

Matilda couldn't contain herself, sobbing uncontrollably she said, "I've been running away for months, sir."

"Would you like to talk, I'm a good listener."

Through her sobs Matilda cried, "I think God's punishing me."

"No, no - why would God want to punish you?"

"Oh sir, some 10 months ago I done a terrible thing. I tried to forget it but ……"

Rev Toby pulled out a clean white linen handkerchief. Matilda blew her nose, sobbing all the more.

"And now God is punishing me for running away from..."

Matilda looked into Reverend Toby's kind face.

"I can't tell you… but I'm not a wicked girl, only done it because…'" Matilda stopped, " I've said too much, I should go."

"Go where?" the Reverend asked.

"I'm unsure, but I'll get a room perhaps in the inn. I've stayed there before, it's ok, that will give me time to think what I'll do... but not now, no not now..."

"You're welcome to stay here for a while."

"No, it's ok, you have been kind but I'd better go."

"What is your name child."

"My name is Mar..., Martha, yes Martha."

The coach pulled into St. Johns, Joseph and Bill thanked the driver.

Martha's Secret

The town was busy with horse drawn carts and people, some carrying heavy sacks on their back, some gentle folk and men in heavy overcoats wearing wide-brimmed hats. Alongside, there are large building, that advertised barbed wire, nails and hammers, another selling boots for gentleman and ladies, boots for riding, an open warehouse where two farriers were working, repairing and making horseshoes.

Joseph and Bill pushed their way through the crowded street to the market. It was buzzing with people buying and selling, the noise was so loud they couldn't hear each other talk. Then Joseph saw Mary Ann, her stall was crowded with women and young girls tugging at the second-hand clothes, holding them up against themselves.

"How much this one?"

"One at a time," Mary Ann shouted, "I'll see to you all."

Joseph pushed his way through to get as close as possible to Mary Ann.

"Excuse me lady."

Mary Ann recognised Joseph.

"You still looking for your friend?"

"Yes I am. Please tell me where to find Rayburn farm."

Martha's Secret

"Go and see Rossie, she works there. Now move along please, I have customers to see to."

"Who's Rosie?" Bill asked.

"I don't know, but I think this lady has had enough of me."

"Excuse me, do you know Rosie?" Joseph asked at a stall holder selling the fresh bread.

"Yes love, she's over there. "Rosie!"

Rosie looked around, "Yes?"

"This young man wants to see you."

Joseph and Bill walked over to her stall.

"Please can you tell me how to get to Rayburn Farm?"

"Hi, I recognise you. You were calling out for Matilda a couple of days ago when we were in the cart. What do you want with her?"

Rosie looked suspiciously towards them.

"Please ma'am, we are her friends. She lived with us at the rectory. She taught the children. We just need to see her."

"Oh, my," Rosie said, "She often spoke of her days at the school. She would never say why she left. Was she in trouble?"

"Oh no, not at all, she had to see a sick aunt."

"Really? she never mentioned a sick aunt to me."

"Please just tell us how to get to the farm?"

"Bit late dearie, she left this morning."

"Left?" Bill spoke for the first time, "Left for where?"

"Look love, I've got lots of customers. I have no idea where she was going. I was hoping she may return to the school but she never said where she was going."

Rosie saw how distressed Joseph looked, "Look love, she only left early this morning. Perhaps someone will know where she's gone. Ask at the coach house or even the inn, now as much as I'd like to help you find her, I must serve these people. I really hope you find her, she's a lovely girl."

Matilda sat quietly in the cathedral watching people coming and going. The two ladies had finished their cleaning.

"Gosh, you still here love?"

Matilda had no idea how long she had been there but her grumbling tummy told her it must be lunch time; she would have loved to buy one of the freshly baked loaves but didn't want to return to the market. Instead, she walked to the inn, pulling her hood over her face so no one could see her black swollen eye or her puffed face, swollen from crying.

"Hello love, haven't seen you for a while? Where you off to with that sack?"

Matilda didn't answer the man at the bar but walked straight to the inn keeper who was laughing and joking with a group of men who had finished their early shift at the timber yard.

"Hello again, what can I do for you?"

"I'd like a room please and something to eat." The inn keeper didn't think to ask why a young women would want a room just two days before Christmas, he just gave her a key.

"Top of the stairs second door along the corridor. I'll get someone to get you a bowl of stew. Where you going to sit?"

Matilda sat hidden away in a corner of the room her back towards everyone. The mutton stew was hot and tasty with a thick slice of fresh bread, a roaring fire was lit in the middle of the bar, the noise of laughter and shouting was deafening but Matilda never turned once to look at anyone.

Bill and Joseph had walked the length of the busy street looking everywhere just hoping to see Matilda.

Martha's Secret

"No mate, no one of that description," the coach driver said as he harnessed his horse, "The other drivers will be in the inn, you could ask them."

Bill had already looked inside the inn but of no avail.

"Let's get a drink," Bill said, "and see if anyone knows anything."

A long bench stood before them packed with people eating their lunch. Bill and Joseph squeezed on the end of the bench clutching a mug of beer.

"I don't feel I can eat anything yet," Bill said, his eyes peering around just hoping and praying he might see Matilda.

Matilda took the last piece of bread to wipe around the bowl, pushing it to the side she picked up her sack and walked towards the stairs to go to her room.

"Matilda! Matilda! oh it's Matilda!"

Joseph jumped up from the bench, pushing his way towards the stairs. At the sight of Joseph, Matilda, gripped with fear, ran up the stairs....

Martha's Secret

"Hey, where do you think you're going," the innkeeper grabbed Joseph's coat.

"Please sir, she is my friend."

"Oh yes, looks like it the way she ran from you."

Bill slipped by, walking up the stairs as if he belonged there. Matilda shut the door but was unable to lock it. Bill knocked.

"Please Matilda, please let me in."

"Go away Mr Stockbrook, just leave me alone."

"Matilda, please let me in, we have travelled to find you. Please let me just talk with you. If you don't open the door, we will be thrown out".

Matilda opened the door just enough to see Bill, "What do you want? Why have you come?"

Bill gently pushed the door open; he tried not to show any reaction on seeing her bruised and battered face.

"Your eye looks sore Matilda. Did you fall?"

Matilda looked into Bill's face, so gentle, so handsome. She didn't answer but tried to pull her hood over to cover up her wounds. Bill walked towards her, gently he pulled the hood away.

"Oh Matilda, what has happened?"

Martha's Secret

The innkeeper taped on the door.

"Everything all right miss?"

"Yes, thank you."

"Well, can this man come in?" Joseph stood excitedly by his side.

"Yes, that's fine."

"Well, you need to know we're a respectable inn; I don't usually allow this."

"We won't stay long." Joseph said, walking into the shabby bedroom. He walked up to Matilda.

"We are so pleased we found you. We have come to take you back,"

Matilda sat on her bed, head in her hands crying out, "I can't come back."

"Why, tell us why" Joseph asked.

"Not while Louisa is there, I cannot come back."

"Lousia? Oh, she left a while ago. She returned to England."

"Oh really, you're not just saying that?"

"No!" Bill said, "she returned to England, but why can't you be with her?"

"Please," Matilda cried, "not now, perhaps one day I'll explain but not now."

"You'll need to pay for the room." Bill put some money on the bar, Matilda held on to Joseph's arm while Bill carried her sack as they left the inn.

"May I go and say goodbye to Rosie?" Matilda asked.

The market was still busy. When Rosie saw Matilda, she left the stall and ran to Matilda, they hugged for what seemed an age.

"Be happy, Tilly."

One last hug and they walked towards the coach house.

"You're lucky," the driver said, "It's only you two gentlemen on this journey, but you must pay for the lady."

"Of course," Joseph said, "and a bit extra for your kindness."

They shared a blanket but spoke little on the journey. Matilda sat gazing out the window, everything seemed brighter and a peaceful feeling, she hadn't felt for a long time came over her.

Chapter 13

Reverend Bullingham was waiting with the pony and trap as the coach arrived. He stepped down to welcome them back, a loving smile was all he gave to Matilda as he helped her onto the trap.

"Soon be back. Mrs B will have a hot meal waiting for us."

"Oh child," Mrs B held Matilda close to her bosom, "what has happened to you?"

"No questions dear." Rev said, "Just a hot meal by the roaring fire please."

"Please may I go and wash and change out of these clothes?"

"Of course, dear, you know your room. Come down when you're ready."

Martha's Secret

The bible was open on the bedside cabinet ... *"Come unto me those who are heavy burdened and I will give you rest."* Matilda fell to her knees, "Thank you dear lord, thank you." After a quick wash and a change of clothes, Matilda joined everyone for a delicious meal. After the meal , Matilda curled up by the fire feeling so contented.

"Well, I have a service to take, hope you're all coming?"

"Oh, I think Matilda should rest."

"No," Matilda said, "I want to come…"

Walking out in the chilly air Matilda could hear the singing from the church.

"Jesus came to bring peace into this troubled world, to reconcile us to God. May you all know the love of Christ this Christmas" Rev said as the service closed. Some of the school children, together with their parents were in the church, after the service children ran up to Matilda...

"Oh Miss, are you back? We have all missed you so much."

One little boy took an unwrapped toffee from his pocket.

"Happy Christmas, Miss Matilda."

As he placed the sticky toffee in her hand, it took Matilda all her self-control not to break down in tears.

"Oh, thank you, Benjamin.

"Oh, miss you remembered my name."

"Yes, and you remembered mine, have a happy Christmas."

Reverend Bullingham stood at the church door wishing folk a blessed Christmas, some put little wrapped gifts into his hand, *'For you and Mrs B.'*

Getting into the clean fresh bed was wonderful, it didn't take Matilda long to fall into a deep sleep. Sitting up Matilda was aware of the silence, she opened her bedroom door, there before her at the bottom of the stairs, stood the grandfather clock. Showing the time…9.45! Matilda washed quickly, dressed and came down to see a bowl of now cold corn mash on the table. Although not very appetising she felt she should eat it. Then she took her dish into the scullery and washed all the dishes soaking in the sink.

"Good morning!" Mrs B came in the door and removed her brightly coloured knitted hat.

"Oh, Mrs B, I'm so sorry I've never slept this long before and I've missed church too."

"There's no need to apologise Matilda you must have been tired after your long journey and then going to the service late last evening."

Joseph walked in with a bag containing a large piece of venison, all ready for the pot. Mr Stockbrook senior had sent it as a gift for Christmas dinner. Mrs B started to peel the vegetables while Matilda got the large pan. The vegetables went on the bottom, then some stock, herbs and finally the venison. Mrs B put it on top of the range.

"That will be a grand Christmas dinner tonight," she said, "along with the plum pudding I made."

Joseph went out in the yard to clear away some of the snow.

"Can I help you Joseph" Matilda asked, already putting her coat and gloves on. Together they cleared the path from the church to the rectory while throwing snowballs at each other at the same time.

"Oh, Joseph," Matilda said, "I didn't think I'd be having such a wonderful Christmas."

"What happened Matilda? I was horrified to see your black swollen eye, and where is your trunk? All you had was a sack with a few bits in."

"Oh, my trunk got stolen and the son of the owner of the farm, well he ….Oh Joseph, it doesn't matter, I'm here now and I'm so happy."

"Well, we better go in and warm ourselves or we will freeze," Joseph said putting his arm into Matilda's.

"Come on in you two," Mrs B said, "There's hot coffee in the pot and a slice of fruit cake."

The fire was roaring, Joseph and Matilda warmed their cold hands by wrapping them around the hot mug of coffee. Reverend Bullingham sat in his armchair reading one of the books Joseph had collected for him. At 3pm the church clock struck, Reverend Bullingham put a thick coat on along with his hat and gloves.

"Come on you two we are meeting up with Bill Stockbrook and some of the children to sing Carol's in the village."

They wrapped up warm, leaving Mrs B to continue with the dinner. When they walked into the church, Bill was already there with 18 of the children.

They walked together to the little village where most the farm workers lived. There they stood in the square giving out Carol sheets to anyone who wanted to join in, singing *'Noel, noel born is the King of Israel...'* Bill came and stood by

Martha's Secret

Matilda sharing her carol sheet, being so close to Bill seemed to warm Matilda inside.

"Would you like to join us for lunch tomorrow, Matilda and you too Joseph?" Bill asked.

Looking at Joseph, they both echoed, "Yes please, we would love to come."

All around the table were pretty Christmas decorations and bowls of delicious food.

"Help yourself to the vegetables," as the bowls were passed around.

Mrs B bought in the venison ready for her husband to carve. What a feast! Reverend thanked God for His provision and for Mrs B cooking it so well.

Matilda knelt by her bed so happy and very tired.

"Thank you, dear lord, for such a blessed day. Please be with my beloved brother and Ma Alice, keep close to us all, and bless Bill Stockbrook. Amen."

Life soon got back to normal after the Christmas celebrations; the children back at school and Matilda enjoying teaching once more.

Chapter 14

Spring was coming with blossom on the trees. It was a warm afternoon; the children had gone home leaving Matilda to pack her books away. Mr Stockbrook arrived and asked if she would like to take a walk with him. Nothing was said for a while then Bill stopped and stepped in front of Matilda, took her hand and looked into her beautiful blue eyes, he stuttered, "I was so worried when you left Matilda. It was such a wonderful day when Joseph and I found you."

"Oh I thank God, Mr Stockbrook that you found me."

"Please Matilda, outside of school, please call me Bill."

Squeezing her hand, still looking into her eyes, "After I lost my wife and baby I never thought I could care for anyone again." Struggling to put his words together he continued.

"Matilda, over these months I..." he stopped, looking away, he asked, "Oh Matilda, do you think you could like me?"

"Oh Mr Stockbrook... Bill, I do, very much," turning towards her again he put his one hand around her waist.

"Matilda, I'm only half a man, but..."

"Oh Bill, there's nothing half about you, you're stronger than many men with two arms."

He lent forward gently pressing his lips against Mathilda's.

"Oh, I'm sorry," Bill said, "that was presumptuous of me. Please forgive me."

Matilda took Bill's hand, "Please don't apologise."

She leant forward and this time pressed her lips hard against Bill's.

"Oh Matilda, you have made me so happy"

Matilda felt feelings she had never experienced before. They continued their walk but this time not a word was spoken.

Life continued with its usual routines in school and the Reverend's household. Bill would visit Matilda Sunday afternoon and, if the weather was pleasant, would drive out in the pony and trap taking a picnic by the lake. Their conversation was mainly about school and the children, Bill longed to ask Matilda what happened that day she left when they found her in the inn with a swollen black eye but something always stopped him from asking.

Matilda would ask about living on the farm, but likewise couldn't seem to ask about his marriage or how he lost his arm. Things came to a head that June afternoon while walking together along the pretty path that led to the village green. Matilda held on Bill's arm, feeling very content and even blessed to have him as a special person in her life. They stopped to sit down on a little bench under a large maple tree. The sun shone the birds were singing, everything seemed perfect... then suddenly Bill got down on one knee.

"My beloved Matilda, my love you must know how I feel about you. I never thought I could find happiness again in my life. Matilda, my love what I'm struggling to say is would you do me the greatest honour of becoming my wife?"

Fear struck Matilda; fear she hadn't felt for long time. She hastily stood up and walked a few steps away, then turning towards the now bewildered man cried,

Martha's Secret

"Bill, I've carried a terrible burden since I arrived in Canada; I try so hard to forget it but it never goes away. Dearest Bill you have bought such happiness into my life and I've become so very fond of you but I cannot marry you."

"Matilda," Bill stood as close to her as she would allow, "tell me this burden that you carry, we can work it out together. I love you!" and taking her hand said "nothing can be so hard we can't sort it out. Marry me, Matilda, Marry me."

"Dearest Bill, I can't tell you because if you knew you would never ask me to marry you. Please, please take me back home now. I am so sorry I never want to hurt you. I love you too Bill very much but because I love you, I must say I can't marry you."

Together, they took a slow unspoken walk back to the rectory. This time there was no parting kiss, Matilda simply walked to the back door leaving Bill standing watching her disappear inside.

"You're back early," Mrs B said, "thought you would have made the best of this beautiful day."

Matilda flung her arms around Mrs B's neck, crying uncontrollably.

"Hey, what's all this about, sit yourself down now what's gone wrong."

"Oh! Mrs B, only if I could tell you; only if I could rid myself of this situation in my life."

"Now you dry your eyes and tell me what's so terrible."

"I can't," Matilda said still sobbing, "I just wish it would go away, but it won't, it can't ever..."

Matilda ran to her bedroom, flung herself on the bed crying into the pillow. She lay alone for what seemed an age before she heard a gentle knock on her bedroom door.

"Matilda, it's me Reverend. Please open the door."

Matilda opened her door and stood looking at Reverend Bullingham, "May I come in Matilda?"

She didn't answer but stepped aside allowing him to come in. He sat on the little wooden chair, Matild sat on the edge of her bed.

"Now, what is all this I have been hearing?"

Matilda put her head down, tears falling onto her lap.

"Nothing, Matilda is ever that bad that the good Lord can't help us with."

"Not this time Reverend, not this time."

He walked over and sat beside Matilda putting a loving arm around her said, "Well let's see, how about telling me this terrible secret?"

"Oh, Reverend I would like to tell you but I can't."

"Well Matilda, may I ask you why?"

"Because you wouldn't want me living here. You may even go to the police."

"Well child, let me the judge of that. Let me tell you no matter what has happened in your young life, I nor Mrs B would ever reject you. Now I suggest you wash your face, come and join us for supper and perhaps we can talk about this later."

Giving her a kiss on top of her head he walked out the bedroom.

"Supper in 10 minutes, now don't be late."

School, the following Monday, was difficult having to pretend everything was normal in front of the children. Matilda couldn't wait for school to finish, packing the books away she glanced over at Bill, thinking how handsome he was; if only things could have been different.

As Matilda entered the back door of the rectory, Joseph was returning from the village shop picking up the mail that had arrived.

"You have a large envelope, Matilda," Joseph said placing the mail down on the table.

Matilda picked up the envelope addressed to her, puzzled at what it could be. She excused herself so she could take it to her bedroom to read.

"Dearest Martha, it's with great sadness and sorrow I write this letter to you. On October 3rd your dear brother Johnathan died of consummation, the funeral was held on October 17th.

I will try to explain everything that happened the weeks before his death. A merchant ship arrived from the Caribbean in August; the captain went along to the police station to report that when they left last time a man named Jacob Morse was missing. Some of the sailors had told him they had been gambling at your father's house. It was then the police visited your brother and told him the case of the fire at his parent's home was being reopened as they suspect the bones they found belonged to this man . They told your brother, that Jacob Morse was a wanted man, who had murdered 3 women after raping them. Your brother felt he needed to explain what had happened and that it was him who poured the paraffin and set fire to the house. At court, it was told how Mr Morse broke into your bedroom intending to rape you in self-defence you pushed him causing him to hit his head on the fireplace, causing his death. That dear one was the statement from your brother. He admitted setting fire to the house out of fear. He was found guilty of arson and sentenced to 12 years imprisonment, but sadly after only five weeks he died of consumption.

The funeral took place 10 days later. Such sad news for you Martha, I am so sorry to have to be the one to have to tell you. The case has now been closed, as far as you are concerned the police are not holding you responsible for Mr Morse's death.

I do hope you have found happiness in Canada and can put to rest this horrid situation you found yourself in.

Be happy I know that's what Johnathan would have wanted for you. I close sending my love to you Ma Alice."

Matilda sat reading and re-reading the letter. Sadness overwhelmed her for the loss of her brother; how sad for him to die alone. Yet at the same time she felt a sense of great release, something that had been with her since that horrid day. Time and time again, she had re-enacted the scene in her bedroom, now somehow it was no longer."

Sitting at the table, Reverend, Mrs B and Joseph listened to Matilda as she told them the whole story. She then passed the letter to the Reverend and asked him to read it out aloud.

They all sat in silence; you could see the shock on Mrs Bs face.

"Well now my dear," Reverend eventually said, "That chapter of your life is now closed but I'm sorry that your brother has died; it must be so sad for you."

"The saddest thing," Matilda said crying, "is I wasn't able to be at his funeral. He was my only family and that's what hurts me."

"Would you like me to do a little service for him here in our chapel?"

"Oh yes please that would be wonderful," Martha lifted her face tears still running down her cheeks, "Thank you Reverend, thank you so much."

"We will do it this Sunday afternoon, Joseph would you make a plaque with Johnathan's name on."

"That would be a privilege" Joseph said.

He went over to Matilda, with his arm around her he said,

"You might not have a brother now, but I've always thought of you as my adopted sister."

"Oh Joseph, that is the kindest thing you could say to me. I love you all as if you where my own family."

"Well now," Mrs B said, "perhaps you will come and help me with the supper, cold ham and potatoes. You dear Joseph can lay the table and we can eat as a family."

Matilda didn't sleep very well that night thinking of Johnathan, wondering if his wife had showed any compassion or even if she had attended the funeral.

Walking into the classroom, she saw Bill was already sitting at his desk marking some of the children's work.

"Excuse me Bill," Matilda tapped on the door and walked in.

"Good morning, Matilda, you are early."

"Yes, I wanted to see you before the children arrived."

"Oh, is there a problem?"

"No not really, but I received news yesterday that my dear brother Johnathan has died."

Bill stood and faced Matilda, thinking how beautiful she was.

Martha's Secret

"Oh I am so sorry Matilda, that is so sad for you being so far away."

"Reverend Bullingham has offered to do a service for him Sunday afternoon and I was wondering if you would come, I'd so love you to be there."

"Of course I'll come Matilda."

"Oh, and when the children have gone home after school may I walk with you?"

"Well yes but..." he never finished his sentence before Joseph was ringing the bell for the children to return to class.

From October until March, school finished at 2pm as some of the children had a half hour walk home and there were days when it was bitterly cold and often snowy. But this day, the sun was shining and no snow! Matilda packed her books away and watched as the children walked out of the classroom.

"Bye, Miss Matilda, see you tomorrow."

"Bye children, straight home now."

Bill put his head round the door, "I'll just get my coat and gloves and I'll be ready Matilda."

Martha's Secret

Walking out of the building, she asked Bill if they could walk towards the lake.

"Bill, I love it there. Do you remember some of those Sunday afternoon walks we had together?"

There before them stood a large bench, the one they used to sit on.

"Can we sit here, please Bill?"

"Is there something bothering you Matilda?"

"For a long time Bill, I haven't been able to share with anyone what happened in my life before I came to Canada but yesterday I received a letter, first about the death of Johnathan but much more."

Matilda moved slightly away from Bill. Bill looked lovingly at Matilda as she told him everything that happened that horrible night. She even told him why she ran away when she saw Louisa, realising she hadn't mentioned that at the rectory.

Bill sat silently not knowing what to say. Matilda then handed him the letter. Bill sat reading all that Ma Alice had written. Matilda got up and walked to the lake's edge. When Bill finished reading, he walked over to Matilda putting his arm around her shoulder.

"Oh, dearest Matilda, only if you had told me."

"I couldn't, I didn't know if one day I'd end up in prison or even hung."

That sent a cold shiver through Bill's body.

"I so wanted to tell you Bill and when you asked me to marry you, I was so afraid."

She looked into Bill's beautiful gentle face, "Oh Bill, could you forgive me? Is there a chance?"

"Bill put his hand on Mathilda's face, "Shhhh, shhhh." Taking his hand away from her mouth he pressed his lips gently on hers.

"Look at me Matilda. I love you; I'll always love you."

"Oh, dearest Bill only…"

"No Matilda, marry me, make me the happiest man in the world."

"Yes, yes a thousand times yes. Oh Bill, this is the happiest day of my life."

Bill held her so close he could feel her heart beating through his coat.

"Come on," he said, "I have something to do."

Holding Matilda's hand they ran back to the rectory.

"What you two smiling about?" Mrs B said, as they rushed through the door.

"I need to speak to the Reverend."

"Matilda, you stay in the parlour with Mrs B."

The door was slightly ajar so that Mrs B made sure she could hear what was being said.

"Reverend Sir, may I speak with you?"

Reverend Bullingham put his book and pipe down.

"Reverend, I've asked Matilda to be my wife and she has agreed. Please sir, I hope you will give us you're blessing."

Reverend Bullingham stood up and shook Bill's hand.

"Bill this is wonderful news and indeed you both have my blessing."

"And mine," Mrs B said rushing through the door.

The memorial service was special. Joseph made a beautiful plaque, *'In loving memory of Johnathan Archibald Turner 1872 – 1900.'* Mrs B put a vase of primroses by the little photo of Johnathan that Matilda had placed by the plaque. Reverend spoke a prayer of thanksgiving for Johnathan's life before they left the church for the rectory for a special tea Mrs B had made.

Matilda looked beautiful in the dress Mrs B had made for her, lace and satin, holding Joseph's arm clutching a small bouquet of pink, white and yellow chrysanthemums. They walked joyfully down the aisle, watched by the children from the school along with their parents.

"Do you take this woman, Martha Matilda Turner to be your lawful wife?"

"I do."

"Do you take this man, William James Stockbrook to be your husband."

"Oh, I do."

The end

Martha's Secret

It would only be right to tell the reader what happened next in the life of Mr and Mrs Stockbrook. They set up home in a small cottage on Mr Stockbrook Senior's farm. Within a year, their first child was born, Johnathan William, a beautiful healthy baby. Two years later, Rosie Matilda was born.

Joseph visited regularly with his young wife Agnes. They continued to live with Reverend Bullingham and Mrs B.

Mr Bill Stockbrook continued as headmaster of the now growing school, with two new teachers Daniel Price and Mary Summers added to staff.

Ma Alice kept in contact with Matilda by writing regularly, and Matilda periodically visited the market at St. Johns to see Rosie and the others to show off her little family.

About the Author

Carol is married to Ian and lives in Essex. Carol has always enjoyed writing, especially short stories, often taken from the Bible, expressed through the eyes of onlookers.

Carol's experiences as a psychiatric nurse and pastor's wife, alongside those gained from mission trips abroad and serving alongside Ian in prison, bring a rich tapestry of life to her writing.

Carol is also a motivational speaker.

For contact: carolbmoore@hotmail.co.uk

Printed in Great Britain
by Amazon